Lord Lindum's Anus Horribilis

By a gentleman

Quirinal Press LN2 5RT

Copyright © Ian Thomson 2020

Ian Thomson has asserted his right under the Copyright, Designs and Patents Act 1988 to be identified as the author of this work

All rights reserved

This book is sold subject to the condition that it shall not, by way of trade or otherwise, be lent, resold, hired out or otherwise circulated without the publisher's prior consent in any form or binding or cover other than that in which it is published and without a similar condition including this condition being imposed on the subsequent purchaser

This book is a work of fiction. The characters within it are not intended to represent any persons, living or dead. Any apparent resemblance is purely co- incidental.

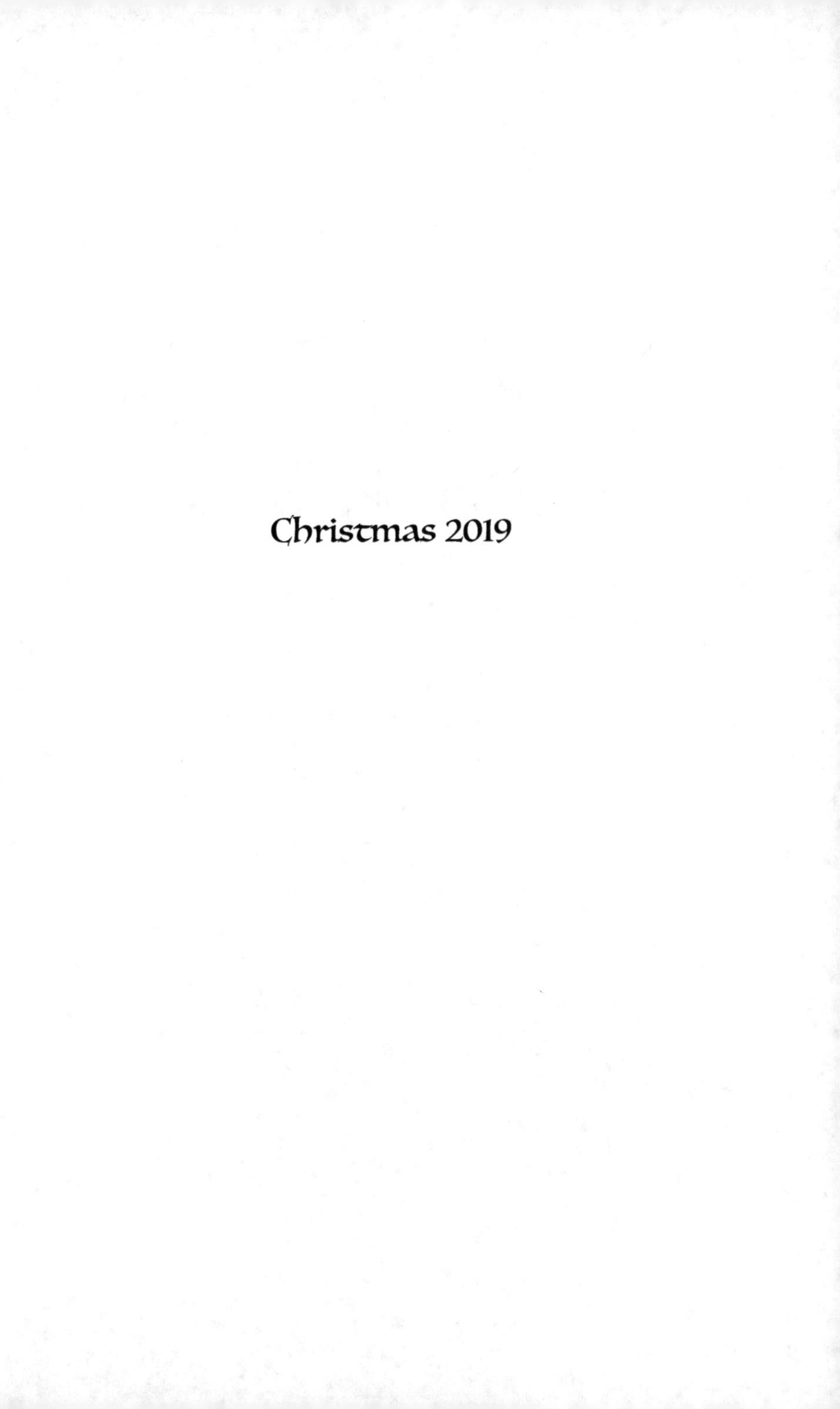
Christmas 2019

'What the deuce do you mean by telling me that I can't have devilled kidneys for breakfast, Fiskerton? Do I employ you to deny me a decent breakfast? What do you mean by it? Eh?'

'With respect, your lordship, I have already explained several times that since it is Christmas Eve, I have many chores to accomplish during the course of the day, if your lordship is to enjoy the festal period to the full.'

'Oh, very well, a dish of kedgeree will have to do, I suppose.'

'Out of the question.'

'A brace of kippers?'

'What I had in mind, your lordship, was toast and jam.'

'Toast and jam! Toast and jam! You expect me to breakfast on toast and jam while you, no doubt, gorge yourself in your pantry on grouse pie and my best claret? You are an unconscionable bounder, sir!'

'I very much doubt if I shall have time to break my fast at all today, my lord. Would you kindly lift up your feet while I get the Dyson under your commode.'

'Eh? What's that? There's a bison under the commode?'

'No, my lord. There, it's done. You can put your feet on the floor again.'

'I wasn't afraid you know, Fiskerton.'

'No, my lord, of course not. Now, I venture to suggest that you might feel somewhat placated, if I say that there is a pot of Lady Birchwood's limoncello marmalade left.'

'Ah, now you're talking, man. Very well, just run my bath for me, if you would.'

'I wonder if, just this once, your lordship might attend to that himself.'

'What? Run my own bath?'

'Indeed, sir.'

'But I don't know how!'

Later

'Your morning coffee, my Lord.'

'Capital, capital, I must say I hardly expected it after the pitiful pother at breakfast. Well, pour it, man, pour it. Don't stand there like a vegan at a carvery. And what pray is this?'

'Stollen cake, your lordship.'

'You've stolen a cake? Is there no end to your knavery, Fiskerton? You'll have us both in chokey at this rate.'

'I hardly think so, sir. It was purchased honourably. It is a yeasted confection filled with dried fruit and almonds and a soupçon of marzipan. It is German in origin, I fancy.'

'Do you expect me to consume something created by A FILTHY HUN?!'

'Calm down, your lordship, or you'll have one of your turns. You have stollen cake every year. You like it.'

'I do?'

'Indeed. Might I suggest you try it? Just a minuscule nibble to begin with?'

[Pause]

'But Fiskerton - this is sublime! Why did you not say so?'

Later still

'Ah, there you are, Fiskerton. Where have you been? Swinging the lead again, I'll be bound.'

'Not a bit of it, your lordship. I have been making a savoury pie for your Christmas Eve dinner; I have polished the silver; I have prepared the vegetables for tomorrow's feast; I have decked the hall with boughs of holly, and I have shaved a sensitive area around the cat's boil to minimise itching.'

'A likely story. Bring me my sherry.'

'Very good, your lordship.'

'What's for luncheon?'

'Smoked oysters on toast, your lordship.'

'More bally rogering toast! I had toast for breakfast.'

'With salad.'

'To blazing hell with your blithering salad! More blasted toast! By the Lord Harry, How dare you offer me more TOAST?'

'Smoked oysters on toast is your favourite, your lordship.'

'Is it? Is it really?'

'It is indeed. And I thought a crisp glass of Muscadet might complement it to perfection, sir.'

'I'm warming to the idea, Fiskerton. Warming to it, I say.'

Much later

'Fiskerton, you poltroon, what are you doing? I was watching that!'

'I am not turning it off, your lordship, merely changing the channel.'

'I won't know what happens now.'

'You watch Peter Pan several times a year. You know perfectly well what happens. Wendy grows up.'

'That's true. I don't like that bit.'

'No, You don't. You do like Carols from King's, however.'

'I do. Is that what's on now?'

'In a moment.'

'Knew a cove once. Bit too interested in choirboys. Frightful stink. Ended up in the clink.'

'I expect he did.'

'Church of England too - not a Holy Roller. I say Fiskerton, I know a limerick about choirboys: There once was a curate of King's…'

'I've heard it, your Lordship. You recite it every year. It is lubricious and somewhat distasteful.'

'You know what I'd do with choirboys, Fiskerton? Hunt them down. Give 'em a decent start and then release the hounds. Tally-ho!'

'I would imagine that you might end up being confined at Her Majesty's Pleasure, just as surely as your unsavoury associate. A glass of madeira, your Lordship?'

'Top hole. Are you going to join me in a jolly old sing along?'

'I shall decline your kind invitation. I find your lordship's rendition of "O Come All Ye Faithful" a little too sensational.'

Even later

'Corking pie, Fiskerton.'
'Thank you, your lordship. One aims to please.'
'And what will you be having?'
'For supper, your lordship?'
'Yes, for supper.'
'Well, if I can find a little time I might have a little bread and cheese, though there are potatoes to peel and borage and sorrel to find for the soup. I am led to believe they are

best gathered at dusk, though I have been so thoroughly engaged that it is now pitch dark.'

'Bread and cheese sounds most appropriate. I'm sure there must be some good cheddar below stairs. Do not touch the Stilton. Since it is Christmas Eve, you may have a glass of cooking sherry. Just the one, you understand. I imagine you will need to rise early tomorrow.'

'Indeed, your lordship, around 2.30 a.m. is my speculation, if your dinner is to be just so.'

'Well. don't stand around gossiping then. Just pour me a glass of port and you may go.'

'Your lordship is too gracious.'

'Oh, Fiskerton...'

'Your lordship?'

'Leave the decanter!'

Christmas Eve, 2019
Very Late

'Fiskerton! Fiskerton! Where the devil are you?
'I'VE FALLEN OVER!'

Christmas Day

'I hope your lordship approved of my little gift?'

'A copy of *A Christmas Carol*? A fine edition, Fiskerton. I am evidently paying you too much. Remind me to dock your wages in January. Were you pleased with your present?'

'Oh indeed, your lordship. More than pleased. I have always wished to have my very own pencil sharpener.'

Boxing Day

'Now, Fiskerton, plump up the cushions and bring up a decent claret. I am minded to spend the day in front of the idiot box.'

'Very good, sir. Shall I prepare a cold collation for luncheon?'

'Yes do. It will serve for supper too. And perhaps a little grazing in between, eh?'

'Indeed, sir. Will that be all, sir?'

'No, Fiskerton, it will not be all. I shall need you to change the channel occasionally and to refresh my glass frequently.'

Later

'Well, that looks very festive, Fiskerton.'

'I flatter myself that I can furnish a tolerable Boxing Day buffet, sir.'

'Capital, man, capital!'

'You might say, sir, that I am "a man that Fortune's buffets and rewards hath furnished with equal thanks".'

'Eh, what?'

'Hamlet, your lordship.'

'Oh, well put a sock in it now, will you? I'm watching Shaun the Sheep.'

December 27th

'I am bored, Fiskerton.'

'Indeed, your lordship?'

'What day is it?'

'I believe it's Friday.'

'Good Lord, how the devil do you know that?'

'It says so on the page of the *Radio Times* that you have open before you.'

'I say! That's damned clever of you, Fiskerton.'

'It pleases your lordship to say so.'

'It does please me. Unlike the *Radio Times*.'

'Might I ask why, my Lord?'

'Because there is nothing on the idiot box today that would stretch the intellect of a mollusc.'

'I was not aware that gastropods are given to watching television, your Lordship.'

'Leave the pleasantries to me, Fiskerton. There's a good chap.'

'Begging your lordship's pardon.'

'Perhaps we could play a board game?'

'Oh, I'd rather not if it's all the same to you.'

'Why not?'

'Too dangerous.'

'Too dangerous? What's dangerous about a game of bally chess.'

'Well, if I may say so, your Lordship has a slight tendency to be rather cavalier with the rules. The rook does not move diagonally and the Queen, although she may move in any direction, cannot leapfrog over other pieces to get to the King.'

'Pish. Peripheral details.'

'When I ventured to point this out, your lordship began to pelt me with walnuts and threatened to attack my manhood with the nutcrackers.'

'Monopoly then?'

'Oh no, your lordship. Last year when I bought Mayfair you threw the board into the fire, offered to roger me with the poker, and dismissed me from your lordship's service.'

'Why are you still here then?'

'You had Mrs Washingborough place an advertisement in the Post Office window the following day. I reapplied for my position that very evening. Under an assumed name.'

'Which was?'

'"Fiskerton", your lordship.'

'And I was taken in by that subterfuge, was I?'

'You were, your lordship.'

'Extraordinary.'

'Quite so.'

'Well, in that case, make yourself useful. Wind up the gramophone, would you? I am minded to alleviate the boredom by listening to my record of the Spice Girls' Greatest Hits. And fix me a pink gin while you're at it.'

December 29th

'You see, Fiskerton, I always say that these days between Boxing Day and the New year are like a month of Sundays.'

'Am I to take it that your lordship's thoughts have taken on a religious tincture?'

'Good God, no! Heaven forbid!'

'Then I am afraid I fail to capture your lordship's meaning.'

'Hated Sundays when I was a boy, Fiskerton. Nothing to do, do you see? Polish your boots, go to chapel, write to mater - and that was it.'

'Ah, I see. You mean you're bored.'

'Remarkably swift on the uptake today, Fiskerton, old boy. I am not just bored - I am bored out of my tree, drowning in tedium, swaddled in ennui.'

'At the risk of causing offence, I did suggest that an entire jug of Bloody Mary for breakfast might leave you a little out of sorts.'

'And every day is just the same. Nothing on the box but repeats and wall-to-wall David Attenborough. All the same. Take today for instance.'

'Yes, your lordship. I am all ears.'

'What day is it, by the way?'

'Sunday, your lordship.'

'There you are! What did I tell you!'

'If I might make a suggestion, your lordship?'

'You can but try.'

'Why don't you get dressed and dash along to The Polecat and pass the time of day with your friends?'

'It's a bloody long time since I "dashed" anywhere, Fiskerton. But it's a thought, old sprout, it's a thought. Run my bath, will you, and lay out my Sunday best? High time young Lindum went a roistering, eh?'

'Indeed, your lordship.'

'Just a minute. Sunday, you say.?'

'Correct.'

'Botheration. Sunday bloody hours. They don't open for ages yet. And my cronies won't be there anyway.'

'Why not?'

'Christmas. Wives won't let 'em out.'

'Then I'm afraid it will have to be Mr Attenborough.'

'Thing about this Attenborough chappie, Fiskerton, is that whenever you turn him on, there's some poor unassuming wildebeest being eaten. Every time. Without fail. You try it. Turn Attenborough on at random, you'll see. It could be lions, or cheetahs, or hyenas or even crocodiles but there'll be a wildebeest being eaten.'

'Your lordship could try The Blue Planet, perhaps?'

'What's that when it's at home?'

'Mr Attenborough and his team film underwater, your Lordship.'

'No, no, it won't do. There'll be some god-forsaken wildebeest that's fallen off a boat being eaten by sharks. You mark my words.'

New Year's Eve

'Will your lordship be making any New Year's Resolutions?'

'Certainly not. Damned foolish idea. Nobody ever keeps 'em beyond January 2nd and then they spend the rest of the year thinking that they are failures. Which they are. Stuff and nonsense.'

'I see.'

'Besides, I can't think of any.'

'Your lordship might think of undertaking a dry January and giving any sponsorship money to charity.'

'Dry January?'

'Yes, one forgoes alcohol for 31 days.'

'I'd be dead within a week.'

'I rather think you might be right.'

'And anyway. Charity begins at home.'

'Come now. Your lordship is a very wealthy man.'

'I am nothing of the kind. Poor as a church mouse. Wasting money on your wages and Washingborough's. I have to wonder, you know, whether I need a housekeeper AND a butler. Damned extravagant. There's a resolution for you. I have resolved that one of you must go. Happy New Year, Fiskerton. Come on, cheer up man! Face like a smacked arse, what?!'

January 2020

Twelfth Night

'Washingborough back yet, Fiskerton?'

'Mrs Washingborough returned to her duties as house-keeper on New Year's Day. She is most grateful for the compassionate leave which you granted for her to spend Christmas with her ailing sister.'

'Without pay, of course.'

'Of course, your lordship.'

'Well, if she's back, why haven't I seen her?'

'You haven't seen her for the last two decades, your Lordship.'

'Why not, for God's sake?'

'Possibly because she's scared stiff of you.'

Epiphany

'Looks a tad cheerless in here, Fiskerton, now that you've taken the decorations down.'

'It does, indeed, your lordship. I thought it prudent.'

'Prudent?'

'Absolutely, your Lordship. And not to put too fine a point on it - safer.'

'Safer? What the devil do you mean?'

'Safer on account of your lordship's recently discovered sport of taking pot shots at the fairy lights with your service revolver.'

'Don't be such a Holy Willie, Fiskerton. Just a bit of harmless fun.'

'Possibly, your lordship, but we shall need a new fairy for the tree next year, notwithstanding.'

January 10th, 2020

'Now look here, Fiskerton, I do think you might stop whingeing. An estate like this needs buckets of moolah if it is to be kept up as my revered forefathers would expect. Plenty of ackers, old turbot. Shekels akimbo, what! You and Washingborough should be grateful that I kept you both on, you know. Had to juggle the accounts a bit there, you know. Had to be creative, what!'

'Indeed, your lordship, Mrs Washingborough and I are absurdly grateful that you were able to retain us both in your employ. Even though it was necessary for you to halve our wages in order for you to do so.'

'Inspired bit of mathematics that, wouldn't you say? Should have got the Nobel Prize for that little calculation. Still, a profit is never recognised in its own country, they say.'

'I am overawed by your wit, your lordship.'

'I can imagine. Now, go and find the secateurs, will you? I fancy my toenails are a little jagged.'

January 15th

'Fiskerton, may I congratulate you on the perfection of my boiled egg?'

'Strictly speaking, it was coddled, not boiled, sir. For precisely five minutes.'

'If I'd wanted a recipe, Fiskerton, I'd have asked for one. Now fetch my bath chair. I fancy some fresh air would do us good. Why that pained look, eh?'

'I am thinking with a measure of dismay of the prospect of pushing your lordship up Steep Hill.'

'But, my dear fellow, it's our favourite route. Good for your thighs, man.'

'No doubt, your lordship.'

January 25th
Burn's Night

"'Fair fa' your honest, sonsie face, Great chieftain o' the pudding-race!'"

'What?'

'"*Fair fa' your honest, sonsie face*"...'

'Stop. Fiskerton, what are you doing?'

'I am serving up your Burns Night Supper, your lordship.'

'Which is?'

'Which is haggis, tatties and neeps and - whisky.'

'Pray translate.'

'Tatties and neeps are potatoes and turnips, your lordship. And haggis is a Scottish dish consisting of a sheep's or calf's offal mixed with suet, oatmeal, and seasoning and boiled in a bag, traditionally one made from the animal's stomach.'

'Why?'

'Because today is the anniversary of the birth of the Scottish poet, Robert Burns.'

'Is that what the doggerel was?'

'Indeed, your lordship. As is traditional I was reciting the northern bard's "Address to a Haggis".'

'He was given to addressing haggises, was he?'

'Very much so, your lordship. And mice.'

'And is that another haggis over your shoulder, Fiskerton?'

'No, your lordship. Those are bagpipes.'

'What are they for?'

'Hootin' and skirlin', your lordship. They are a musical instrument.'

'Play. No. NO! STOP! What a racket. Now, Fiskerton, you listen here.'

'Your lordship?'

'Take this fetid abomination and hurl it in the pig bin. Grill me a nice piece of fillet steak. As for the bagpipe thing, put a stake through its heart and bury it at the crossroads.'

'Sir.'

'And Fiskerton…'

'Your lordship?'

'Leave the whisky.'

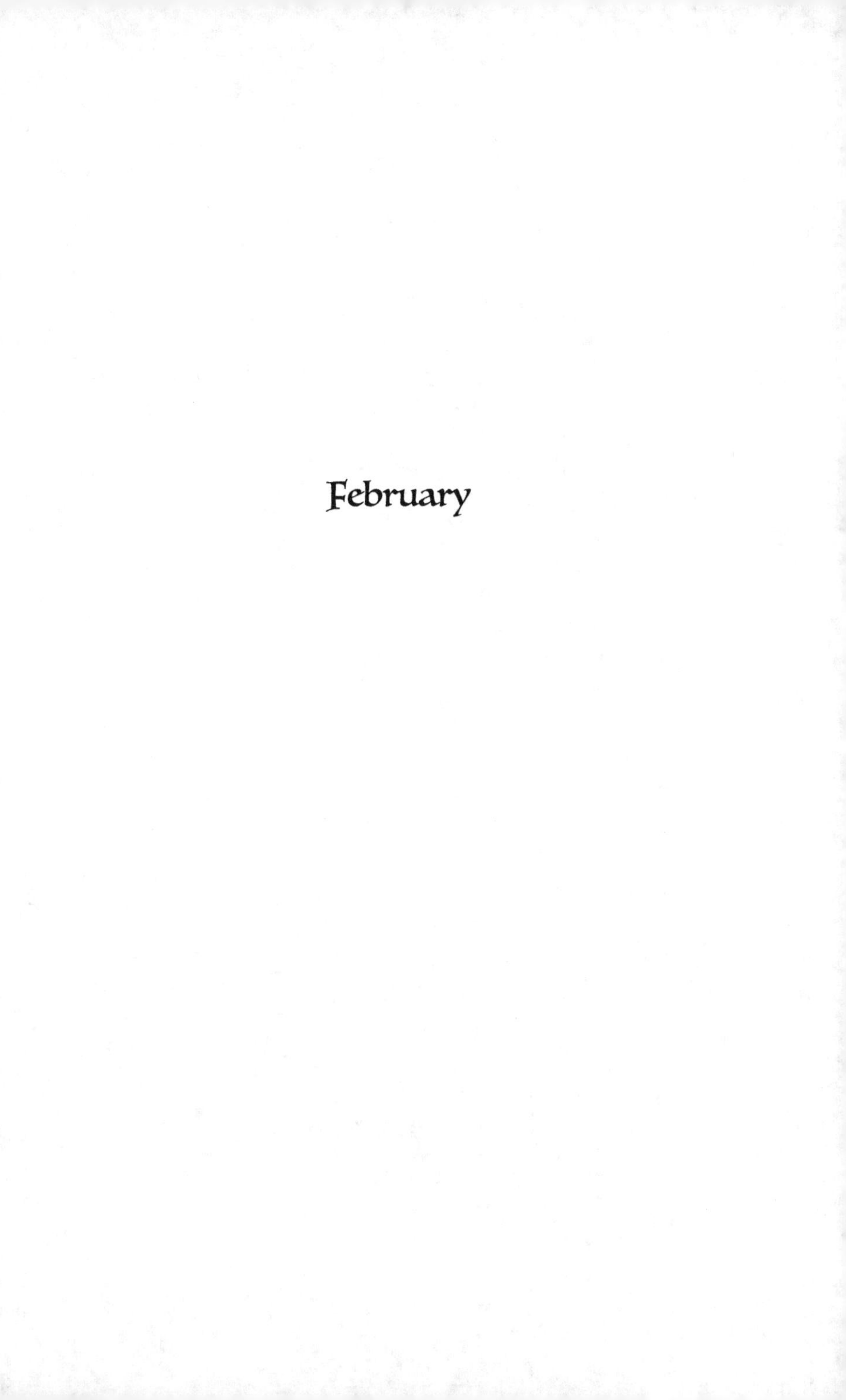

February

ebruary 15th

'What is this bally newspaper blathering on about, Fiskerton. "Coronavirus in China", eh? What is it? Is it like Chop Suey?'

'Well, if your lordship had the patience to read on, you would discover that it is a particularly nasty virus which emerged in China and is spreading rapidly.'

'Like influenza?'

'Exactly, your lordship, only much, much worse.'

'Is it worse than piles?'

'It attacks the lungs rather than the fundament, I believe. To the best of my knowledge, there are no recorded instances of anyone dying from haemorrhoids, though of course I am no expert.'

'No, Fiskerton, you are not. You are a finicky know-all, but you are not an expert. I, on the other hand, am a pundit on the Grapes of Wrath, the Fruits of Tartarus, or as one might call them the Berries of Gehenna. Dammit, man, I haven't been able to sit down for more than two minutes together all day. If only I'd listened to my mother.'

'Was she a sufferer, your lordship.'

'No, you poltroon. Or rather I don't know. I mean, it's not a question you ask of a lady, let alone your own mother, now is it? "Excuse me, ma'am, are you troubled by the piles?" That would never do, would it, you knucklehead. Have you no manners?'

'It would indeed be uncouth to pose such a question. I merely wondered why you invoked the memory of the late and much-lamented Lady Lindum.'

'Because the old bat used to say to me when I was a child: "Don't sit on that cold step, Aubyn, dear. You'll get piles."'

'Well, wasn't she correct in some measure, your lordship?'

'No she was not correct. You don't get piles from sitting on cold steps, you get chilblains.'

'And is your lordship afflicted with chilblains, may I ask?'

'Ye Gods, man, do you think piles and gout are not enough?'

'They are more than enough, your lordship. One cannot but be impressed by the way in which your lordship suffers with the patience of a martyr.'

'That, man, is the unvarnished truth.'

'You were speaking of your lady mother?'

'Ah yes. On other occasions, she might find me standing with my back to the drawing room fire. Now, how else is a gentleman to stand, let alone a peer of the realm, without an arm along the mantel shelf and his arse to the fire? "Aubyn," she would quack, "don't stand there like that. You'll get piles." You have something to say, Fiskerton?'

'Not at all. Pray do go on.'

'I thought you were going to tell me that Mama must have been right?'

'Wouldn't dream of it.'

'Good. Because she wasn't right. She was wrong. If she'd been right I would have got piles at school as a result of the roasting, d'you see?'

'The roasting?'

'Ah, yes, I'd forgotten quite how ill-bred you are, Fiskerton, old potato. Well, in ancient times, when I was but a sprog, long before everything became nancified, discipline in any decent public school, or even in an indecent one like mine, was maintained by the older boys. The masters were either too decrepit, too inebriated, or too infatuated with the Head Man's secretary, Mavis Enderby, to take control. Mavis was known as 'the school bus' because she would give a ride to anyone in the school community and offered 'transports of delight' - allegedly.

'Anyway, the prefects were empowered to beat us savagely.'

'I marvel that your lordship permitted his person to be abused in such a degrading manner.'

'We endured, old halibut, because we knew that in the fullness of time, our own dazzling epoch would dawn and that it would then be our turn to thrash the little shavers in the forms below us.

'Now roasting was for very serious misdemeanours such as brewing a prefect's tea too weak or too strong or failing to buff his shoes to a mirror shine. For that sort of thing offending boys would be stretched out with their backs to the fire and their poor bums close to the glowing coals.'

'Good heavens, your lordship must have displayed consummate fortitude!'

'I did. However, Aubyn De'Ath, future Baron Lindum, developed a ruse which spared him the agonies of lesser creatures who would display the blisters on their *glutei maximi* in the dorm when the roasting was over.'

'And what was this ruse?'

'As I waited in the corridor outside the Prefects' Common Room, I would stuff a number of muffins down the back of my trousers. Thus when the ordeal by fire was over and I was permitted to retire to my study, the muffins were toasted to perfection and my nether cheeks suffered no more than a not unpleasant tingling.'

'I am lost in wonder, love and praise.'

'Of course you are, Fiskerton, of course you are. Now look here, I doubt if I am going to be able to sit down at all today. Run along and get Washingborough to supply you with some of that green ointment. It afforded some relief last time I had a flare-up.'

'Ointment, your lordship?'

'Yes, ointment, you ninny. Stop repeating what I say and get me some ointment.'

'Forgive me, your lordship, but I may be a little while. The unguent in question is Mrs Washingborough's own preparation and I shall have to gather various constituents: hellebore, hemlock and nightshade from the herb garden, for instance - and I must check the mousetraps...'

'Yes, yes, yes. I do not require a catalogue of ingredients. Just get it. Oh and Fiskerton.'

'Your lordship?'

'Throw another log on the fire before you go. I am minded to indulge in a little nostalgia while I wait.'

February 15th

'I have just heard on the wireless that the Department of Health has declared the coronavirus a "serious and imminent threat to public health", your lordship.'

'Do I permit you to listen to the wireless, Fiskerton?'

'You have mandated it, sir, especially during your morning nap. I am to report to you anything you might have missed while in the arms of Morpheus.'

'Ah yes. Continue.'

'It may well be that incomers to our shores will have to be quarantined.'

'I thought that was just for animals.'

'It may have to apply to humans too.'

'Well, I have no objection to cats and dogs and Johnny Foreigner being detained in the interests of public health.'

'It may have to apply to Britons returning from holiday too.'

'No, no, no. That can't be right. You see, "Her Britannic Majesty requests and requires all those to whom it may concern to allow the bearer to pass freely without let or hindrance." An Englishman may come and go as he pleases, you know, Fiskerton. Stand to attention when I speak of Her Britannic Majesty, man.'

'I believe that it is insufficient merely to utter the form of words, your lordship. One must have a valid passport.'

'Do I not have a passport?'

'You permitted it to expire. Your lordship has not been abroad since 1952.'

'I've been to Wales.'

'Wales is not considered to be abroad. A passport is not deemed necessary.'

'Even though they speak a different language?'

'Notwithstanding.'

'I've been to Harrogate.'

'Harrogate is in England, my lord.'

'Is it? Is it? They speak funny there too, you know.'

'Indeed, they do. Shall I bring your elevenses?'

'Yes, do. I could have sworn Harrogate was abroad.'

'There is talk of pancakes on the wireless, Fiskerton.'

'I am not in the least surprised, your Lordship.'

'And why not, *vieux légume*, why not?'

'Because today is Shrove Tuesday.'

'Is it? Is it now? And are we to have pancakes, my old sewer rat? Are we?'

'We are indeed, your lordship, Mrs Washingborough has already mixed the batter and it is resting in the still room as we speak. However, it will fall to me to cook them.'

'Really, Fiskerton, why is that?'

'She is somewhat timorous about the tossing, your lordship.'

'Is she now?'

'Decidedly faint-hearted.'

'Is she? I say, Fiskers, do you think I might have a bash at it?'

'At what?'

'The tossing.'

'Oh, I really don't know, your lordship.'

'What don't you know, damn you? You don't think *me* timorous, do you? You don't consider *me* faint-hearted? You are not accusing the fourth Baron Lindum of being pigeon-livered, are you, you scrote? I'll have you horse-whipped!'

'No indeed, your lordship. That would be quite preposterous. I would never suggest such a thing. It is just that tossing a pancake is something of an acquired skill.'

'Then I shall acquire it. I shall have pancakes with my afternoon tea, Fiskerton, and I shall toss the blighters myself. I will see you in the kitchen at four o'clock sharp.'

'As your lordship pleases.'

Later
The kitchen at Lindum Towers

'Hot steaming tripes, Fiskers, I haven't been down here since I was knee-high to a dung beetle. Rum sort of place, isn't it? Where's Washingborough.'

'I had to administer a paper of sedative and bid her retire to her parlour, your lordship. She was reduced to quivering terror at the prospect of your lordship's appearance.'

'Woman's a fool. Now, where do I start with these pancakes?'

'If your lordship would permit me to demonstrate?'

'Yes, yes, man. Get on with it!'

Fiskerton pours batter into the pan which is already hot and tosses a pancake.

'I say, Bravo, old lollipop, jolly good show! Right now, out of the way man. My turn. Pour the batter. Here goes!

'Oh dear.'

'It is of no consequence, your lordship. I shall scrape it off the ceiling later.'

'Another one. Come on, pour the batter, man. Tally-ho! Yikes! I say, Fiskerton, that really suits you. It may be a rotten pancake but it makes for a rather dashing toupée.'

'Very droll, your lordship.'

March

'FISKERTON! Where the devil is the nincompoop?'

'Immediately behind you, your Lordship. I came at your call.'

'Well, I wish you wouldn't creep up on me like that, man. Bloody rum behaviour. Enough to give a chap the screaming shits.'

'Please accept my most profound and abject apologies, your Lordship.'

'Yes, yes. Blah blah blah-di blah. Now look here, man. What is all this nonsense about a shortage of bog paper? It's all in *The Daily Telegraph*, you see. Nation's going doo-lally.'

'Well, your Lordship, should the worst come to the worst, you might have to have recourse to *The Daily Telegraph*.'

'Are you suggesting that I apply *The Daily Telegraph* to my bottiferous regions?'

'Well, your Lordship, it was meant as a pleasantry but it could be argued that the political orientation of the *Telegraph* is more akin to your Lordship's philosophy than other journals and that its application to your Lordship's undercarriage might be rather 'softer' than, shall we say, *The Daily Mirror*?'

'Hot steaming latrines! Don't give me that crap, Fiskerton! I will not be polishing me ring with a newspaper. How are we for the real thing? Proper lav paper?'

'I daresay the household could survive a month or so on current stocks.'

'Not good enough. Stockpile! Scour the land for every scrap of the stuff - quilted preferably!'

'But is that fair on the proletariat, your Lordship?'

'I don't give an archbishop's teat about the proletariat. The peasantry must use twigs and leaves as they used to before that fool Gladstone gave them ideas. Now off you go. Every scrap, remember - and, yes, three-ply at least - oh, and with puppies.'

'I will endeavour to procure what lavatory paper I can, your Lordship.'

'I should think so. Oh, and Fiskerton...'

'Your Lordship?'

'Make sure you iron it.'

March 11th

'WHO has declared the coronavirus outbreak a pandemic, your lordship.'

'I don't know, Fiskerton, who has?'

'WHO.'

'Who?'

'WHO.'

'Don't stand there too-witting like a blithering owl, you jackass, what on earth are you hooting about?'

'W.H.O. - the World Health Organisation. It was announced on the wireless while you were snoozing.'

'Dash it and darn it. A chap has forty winks and the whole bally world goes to pot. I think I'll have just the tiniest glass of Calvados to keep the spirits up, eh, what? Oy, not *that* tiny! Any other news.'

'The Duke and Duchess of Sussex have performed their last royal duty.'

'Just as well that. A great pity all the same. I thought the Markle girl might bring a bit of new blood to the firm. Fine derrière. But no, I smelt a rat when they named their boy 'Archie'. That's no name for a royal prince. Prince Archie? Sounds absurd. Archie is a name for cats - or butlers, eh what? What did you say your christian name was, eh, Fiskerton? Archie was it?'

'Very jocular, your lordship.'

March 16th

'What will be the consequences of this so-called 'lockdown' then, Fiskerton?'

'It appears that the government will be asking all persons over the age of seventy to cease from social contact for at least twelve weeks, your lordship.'

'Am I over seventy, Fiskerton?'

'I believe your lordship is eighty-two, or thereabouts.'

'How old are you, Fiskerton?'

'I have no idea, your lordship.'

'Excellent. In that case, you will still be able to fetch and carry for me when I am placed under house arrest.'

'Very good, my lord.'

'Meanwhile…'

'Meanwhile, sir?'

'Meanwhile, I must sally forth to the old Polecat to meet up with my chums whilst I can. I'll go tomorrow. And send Scopwick to Lady Skellingthorpe to say I shall be paying her a visit on Thursday.'

'Very prudent, if I may say so. I venture to think we may be in this for the long haul, your lordship.'

'You venture to think? I don't pay you to think, Fiskerton. You may go. Make sure my shoelaces are pressed for tomorrow.'

Later

'There appears to be no sherry, Fiskerton.'

'I believe Mrs Washingborough has made a trifle, sir.'

'But Washingborough knows I despise trifle.'

'I believe it is destined for the Servants' Hall, sir.'

'With my bally sherry? Very well bring me a whisky and soda with no soda.'

March 18th

The Servants' Hall

Lindum Towers

'I should imagine he will be very poorly when he wakes up, Mr Fiskerton.'

'Indeed, Mrs Washingborough, I should not care to be him when he does. He has been asleep for the better part of thirty-six hours.'

'What exactly happened?'

'I received a telephone call at about two o'clock yesterday morning. It was his lordship demanding that I collect him from The Polecat instanter. He had been carousing with his cronies since noon the previous day.'

'How disgraceful.'

'That is not for us to say, Mrs Washingborough. Pray, remember your place.'

'I am so sorry, Mr Fiskerton. I did indeed forget myself for a moment there.'

'We'll let it pass, shall we?'

'I should be grateful.'

'Well now. I drove his lordship to The Polecat in the morning and saw him installed on his habitual stool in the corner of the little snug bar. His intimates were already there and they assisted me in getting his lordship out of the car and through the lounge to the snug where he is accustomed to hold court. Present were Colonel Swinethorpe, Sir Hubert Grange de Lings, Canon Scothern and the younger Mr Hykeham. These gentlemen made merry at my expense but I know my place and left them to their libations.

'In the small hours of the next morning, when I was summoned to collect his lordship, I had some trouble starting up the Bentley as Scampton does not have the time to maintain it properly, what with his duties as gardener, woodsman, gamekeeper, groom, chauffeur, estates manager, carpenter, and general handyman. At last it coughed itself into life and I set off for the village.

'I could hardly believe my eyes as I approached The Polecat. The headlights revealed the horrid spectacle of his lordship and his friends *dancing* on the village green, to the tune of Canon Scothern's penny whistle. It was a devilish sight - and the canon a man of the cloth too!'

'But, Mr Fiskerton, his lordship is wheelchair bound?'

'Aye, when it suits him, he is. I have sometimes settled him in his armchair by the drawing room fire and returned twenty minutes later to find a decanter of brandy, which I had filled only an hour before, quite empty, despite the sideboard being at least fifteen yards from the fire. But this must remain strictly *entre nous*.'

'Of course. But tell me, Mr Fiskerton, is his visit to Hartsholme House to proceed.'

'It is, though I consider it ill-advised. Young Scopwick was despatched to inform Lady Skellingthorpe that his lordship wished to pay her a visit and her ladyship has replied that he will be most welcome. She writes that she has chosen to forget the incident at Bath in 1973.'

'Oh dear, I fear no good may come of it.'

'My good woman, I must confess that I share your foreboding.'

March 19th
Hartsholme House
Seat of Hippolyta, Dowager Countess of Skellingthorpe

'Hippo, you ravishing creature! 'Tis I! Come to brighten this umbrageous morning for you!'

'Aubyn, you revolting rascal. You look atrocious. Whatever is the matter? You look as if a blind person had reassembled your face. Wheel him here by the fire, Fiskerton. That's right.'

'Bit of a bender with the fellows down at The Polecat earlier in the week. Not quite recovered yet.'

'Same old bounder, eh? Well, we must do something about that, mustn't we? Hair of the dog, eh? Whole pelt of the thing eh? Hackthorn, champagne for his lordship - *[aside]* - Cooking champagne will do. His lordship won't

know the difference - *[to Lord Lindum]* - Are you comfort-
able, Aubyn?'

'I most certainly am, come and sit by me, my treasure.
Fiskerton, pull up that pouffe for her ladyship. No, not Hackthorn, you dolt. I am referring to the article of furniture.'

'Thank you, Fiskerton. Hackthorn, take Fiskerton below
stairs with you. Mrs Potterhanworth will look after him. And
hurry up with the bubbles before his lordship perishes from
thirst.'

Much later

'Well, dearest Hippo, that was a frightfully spiffing
luncheon.'

'Well, I know you're partial to a spot of game pie, Aubyn, and Potterhanworth always does one proud in the pie
department. Bagged the birds myself, of course - and the
hare - had to get the venison from the butcher though. My
stag hunting days are over, alas. Because of the dropsy, you
know.'

'It was a pie to marvel at, my old sweetmeat, much better than that ghastly offering we had at Sandringham all
those years ago.'

'Oh, Christ-on-a-bike, I'd forgotten about Sandringham!'

'They never did invite us back, did they?'

'Well, I should think not after your behaviour.'

'It wasn't my fault. I thought the girl was one of the waitresses.'

'Well, she wasn't. You only went and goosed one of those superfluous princesses.'

'Well, I wasn't to know that, was I? She was wearing what I thought was a maid's headdress. Turns out it was one of those fornicators.'

'Fascinators.'

'That's the jobbie. Bloody fatuous kind of titfer, if you ask me. Duke of York came after me with a damn twelve-bore, if I remember rightly.'

'He did. You zoomed across the lawn, pursued by foot-men, at one hell of a lick. How we laughed.'

'I was a tad more fleet of foot in those days, my old sturgeon. Had to climb a bally tree in Sandringham church-yard before they called off the chase. Mind you, I seem to remember you blotted your copy book too, Hippo.'

'I did rather. We were playing charades in the White Drawing Room and I'm afraid I'd knocked back a few gallons of the old claret at dinner. I was performing a rather lewd mime meant to represent Dicken's *Hard Times* when I passed out. I've been *persona non grata* ever since.'

'I say, Hippolyta, what is that ghastly smell?'

'Oh dear, it's Dido, the pug. She's getting on a bit, you know, and tends to break wind rather promiscuously when she's sleeping.'

'Great galloping gooseberries! What do you feed the creature? Carrion? Sulphur? Pig manure? By the worm that never dies, that is rank!'

Her ladyship sprays the sleeping dog from a cut glass scent bottle.

'That's no good, woman. You're not going to get rid of that mephitic pong with lily of the valley. Ring for Fiskerton immediately. I need to get out of here post haste. Help! *Au secours!* I am being gassed, I tell you.'

'Aubyn, will you stop spinning around in that wheel-chair. Now look what you've done. You've run over darling Dido.'

'Is it dead?'

'I don't think so. But she's gone very quiet.'

'It can't be dead - unless it's farting posthumously. Ah, Fiskerton, there you are. Get me out of here pronto!

April

April 1st

'Now, remind me again, Fiskerton, what does Her Majesty's Government permit, and what does it disallow?'

'With certain exceptions, people are prohibited from leaving their own homes.'

'That is no very great inconvenience and after our luncheon at Hartsholme House it may be no bad thing.'

'Indeed, sir.'

'Did the dog die?'

'No, my lord, though I understand it has a very pronounced limp.'

'I see. Well, go on, man, what else?'

'Places of worship are to be closed.'

'I say, that's a bit ripe, wouldn't you say? What happens if a fellow wants to be married or christened? What happens if a chap wants to be buried?'

'It's not permitted, your lordship.'

'Well, you and I had better hang on a bit longer then, hadn't we, you old coffin dodger? We'll have to cock a snook at the grim reaper, eh what?'

'Restaurants, cafés, cinemas and theatres must close.'

'No skin off my nose. Horrible phoney bourgeois holes. Full of the affected middle classes with their pretentious tastes and spoilt kids. Smashed avocado, skinny latte, theatre of the oppressed, film noir - load of hairless bollocks. I rest my case. What else?'

'Pubs must close.'

'I say, steady on. Is this some kind of April fool caper? You can't fool me, you know!'

'I fear it is the stark truth, your lordship. On the other hand, it may be just as well that time must elapse before your lordship's next visit to The Polecat. I am given to understand that your lordship's jocundity and the revelry of your lordship's intimates was not universally well-received, least of all by mine host, Major Saxilby.'

'You have a point. What other miseries must we endure.'

'One may leave one's home for one form of exercise per day.'

'Well, that's splendid. You can take me for a spin in my bath chair each morning after breakfast.'

'With the greatest respect and reverence, your lordship, whilst I can see that I shall be greatly exercised by this scheme (if not rendered wholly prostrate), I fail to see how your lordship will be taking any exercise at all.'

'Don't be spiteful, Fiskerton. It doesn't suit you. Is there anything else?'

'Gyms are to close.'

'Hardly heart-breaking.'

'As you say, my lord.'

'Afraid my sporty days are over, Fiskerton. Once upon a time I was a bit of a whiz at cricket. Best in my house at school - bar one - a nancy boy called Ashby de la Launde. He had a nauseating crush on some dim tart from the Remove. He was regularly beaten up for it by the school bully, Boothby Graffoe, but it failed to straighten him out. I don't know if it was because he was bent but he could bowl a devastatingly devious googly.

'And then, of course, I became a wizard of the croquet lawn at the varsity. Used to play here often, at Lindum Towers, if you remember.'

'I do indeed, your lordship. I recall one occasion in particular when your lordship struck Lady Skellingthorpe over the head with your mallet.'

'Ah yes, a memorable day. I fear she never completely recovered.'

'There was something I didn't quite understand, your lordship.'

'Pray what was that, retainer of meagre understanding?'

'It is just that the countess was your partner on that occasion.'

'That is the case and the fact is that the useless (albeit titled) bint had just performed a roquet of exceptional ineptitude which cost us the game. Do you understand now?'

'What in the name of Beelzebub do you call this, Fiskerton?'

'I don't call it anything, your lordship. It's dead - and cooked to boot. It isn't customary to grace a dish of meat with a name.'

'But it's not lamb.'

'Evidently not. Especially given that it has two legs and wings - not usually ovine characteristics.'

'It's a chicken!'

'Glory be, so it is!'

'I hope for your sake you are not presuming to patronise me, Fiskerton.'

'Certainly not, your lordship. The idea!'

'But I always have lamb at Easter.'

'There was none to be had, your lordship.'

'None to be had?'

'Indeed not. There are many commodities which are quite simply unobtainable because of the pestilence. Things like flour, bread, rice, pasta, baked beans, tinned tomatoes, eggs and hot cross buns. I sent young Scopwick to scour the county on his bicycle but to no avail.'

'I missed the hot cross buns and eggs at breakfast and now there is no lamb, just poultry.'

'Try to think of it as the Paschal Chicken, your lordship.'

'Don't be ridiculous. Carve the thing, will you? I've lost the will to live.'

Later

'What are you saying, you vacuous vassal? Her Britannic Majesty addressed the nation on the idiot box and you didn't wake me! Do you value your nadgers, man?'

'I tried to wake your lordship but it was impossible, conceivably as a result of the two bottles of Pouilly Fuissé which your lordship consumed with the chicken and the half-bottle of port which accompanied the Lincolnshire Poacher cheese. You roused yourself at one point to sing that it was your 'delight on a shining night, in the season of the year' (though what you claimed your delight was, on the aforementioned shining night, I could not bring myself to repeat).

'Then your lordship passed out again and, had you not muttered some fragments of what I took to be a salacious limerick concerning the Bishop of Birmingham, I might have assumed that you had expired.'

'Yes, yes, yes. But what did Our Sovereign Lady have to say.'

'In brief, she expressed her profound sympathy and solidarity with her people and concluded with "We will meet again".'

'Her Britannic Majesty *sang*? Her Majesty sang that glorious song made popular as an Ode to Hope by the resplendent Vera Lynn? I would have given my estates to have heard Her Majesty *sing*.

And you made me miss it! Take your pasty face below stairs. I very much doubt if I shall ever speak to you again.'

'I think your lordship may have mistaken my meaning...'

'DEPART!'

May

 *ay 16th*
VE Day

The Servants' Hall
Lindum Towers

'Mrs Washingborough, I am not certain I can take any more. His lordship is always demanding but today I am beginning to doubt my sanity. His lordship's was a lost cause long ago, of course. How is the bunting going? Are his instructions clear?'

'Oh yes, I am to make as much red, white and blue bunting as I can. When I asked you to take a note to him to say that I was running out of fabric, his reply was that I was to use the bed linen from all the guest bedrooms and dye it appropriately. He writes that we haven't had guests for donkey's years, which I suppose is true. When was there last a house party at Lindum Towers, Mr Fiskerton?'

'The Queen's Silver Jubilee in 1977. We had quite a houseful, I remember, and it began well enough, but in the end pretty well all the guests vowed they would never set foot in the place again. What with the black face soap, whoopee cushions and foaming chamber pots, most found it rather a trial. The Marquess of Spilsby did not appreciate the earthworms in his bed and the Marchioness had a fit of the vapours on encountering a tarantula in her jewellery box. It was plastic, of course, but she wasn't to know that. I am afraid his lordship's sense of humour never quite progressed beyond the dormitory japes of his schooldays.

'But it was the random bottom-tweaking, irrespective of age, gender or rank, that caused many to take to their carriages and flee. Only Lady Skellingthorpe remained until the weekend was over. She rather likes to be tweaked I fancy.

'Now, Mrs Washingborough, I do wish I could persuade you to take your instructions from his Lordship in person. This running up and downstairs with written messages is rather farcical, you know.'

'Oh please, don't bring that up again, Mr Fiskerton. You know it distresses me. I would rather starve naked in a ditch in a thunderstorm and die of Covid-19 alone in the night than go upstairs. Just hearing his lordship squeaking along the corridors in his wheelchair gives me palpitations and when I hear him bellowing at you over my head, I cannot hold my water for fear. Please don't make me go upstairs.'

'Oh, very well. As you wish.'

'Oh thank you, Mr Fiskerton. Thank you and bless your kind heart. I am quite happy down here working my fingers to the bone on this here bunting.'

'Has his lordship left any further instructions for you?'

'Well no, but there is a strange message with a direction for you at the end. Here, look. I can't make head nor tail of it. It says:

Tell Fiskerton:

HANG OUT THE BANNERS

ON THE OUTWARD WALLS

'Ah, I think you'll find that that comes from the Scottish play. He studied it at his public school and quotes it often. Who would have thought that a play about a homicidal maniac would have etched itself on his lordship's mind so deeply? But I must bestir myself. It is almost time to take up his lordship's breakfast.'

'Where is his lordship, Mr Fiskerton? It is strangely quiet above stairs this morning.'

'On the roof.'

'On the roof?'

'I am afraid so. He rang for me just before dawn and said he intended to spend VE Day on the roof, virus or no virus. He said that he was going to show the county how a man of quality celebrates the Empire's Victory over Fritz. Fortunately, the weather is clement but I don't mind telling you, it was the devil's own job getting his lordship's wheelchair up those narrow steps with his lordship in it, shouting and waving his walking stick about.'

'But how on earth did you manage it?'

'With great difficulty and I fear I may have done my back in. I had to summon assistance from Scampton and Scopwick.'

'Scopwick! But his lordship won't have the boy in the house because of the smell.'

'It would help, would it not, if his lordship didn't insist that the lad sleep in the piggery? He says it's because the boy stinks and I tell him that the boy stinks *because* he has to sleep in the piggery and we just go round in circles getting nowhere. Anyway we hosed him down before we let him indoors.'

'But there's another thing, Mr Fiskerton. Him and Scampton shouldn't be in the house at all, because of the virus.'

'Oh, don't you worry about that. His lordship had thought it all through. He made me dig out some World War II gas masks from a box in the cellar. They were something of a serious inconvenience as we tried to manoeuvre the wheelchair up the stairs and I must say the boy looked like a rather thin baby elephant in his mask.'

'But why does his lordship want to be up there at all?'

'My dear Mrs Washingborough, you may very well ask. I only know that while his lordship is breakfasting we must begin putting up the bunting around the outside of the house.'

'But his lordship will not be able to see it from the roof.'

'Quite so.'

'And the nearest building is ten miles away.'

'His lordship is untroubled by the fact. He thinks that because he can see Lincoln Cathedral in one direction and Boston Stump in another, the whole county can see Lindum Towers. He has also insisted that the union flag be flown today though he will not suffer his baronial flag to be lowered so I shall have to erect another flagpole.'

'His lordship's banner is rather beautiful, Mr Fiskerton, you must admit. I like to see it as I take the turning from the village.'

'Must I admit it? I suppose a polecat rampant argent on a field azure, quartered with beetroot gules on a field vert, is quite striking.'

'Pity there'll be nobody to see it, what with Lindum Village being behind the only hill in these parts.'

'It is possible the villagers may be able to *hear* his lordship, however.'

'What on earth can you mean?'

'He had me manhandle his old gramophone up there and has been playing *There'll be bluebirds over the white cliffs of Dover*, *We'll meet again* and *Lili Marlene* since dawn. He's also been reciting poetry through a megaphone, including Binyon's *They shall not grow old*. I fear that he has rather confused VE Day with Remembrance Sunday.'

'He always had a very slender grasp on reality.'

'That is true, Mrs Washingborough and very well put. He believes that the Red Arrows will be forming a special fly past just for him at 13 hundred hours. And this evening he is going to let off some fireworks, if you please, also rescued from the cellar, where they had slept in peace for years - since the millennium celebrations in fact. It is a matter for concern and I fear he might do himself a mischief.'

'You had better have some breakfast before you take him his kippers.'

'No time, I'm afraid. He has a case of Champagne up there with him and I fear the worst. It is going to be a very long day.'

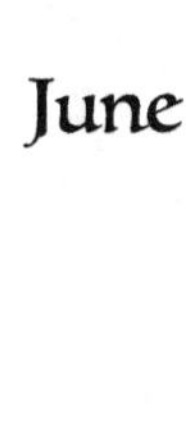

J une 6th

'Oh! Aaaaargh! Ouch! Eeek! Oh, God's bowels! AAAAARGH! Careful you bonehead!'

'With respect, your lordship, it is extremely difficult to dress your lordship's foot while you are wriggling.'

'Oh, jumping Jehosophat! Have you no heart man?'

'I must say that your lordship's suffering is indeed a pitiable sight but I can do nothing to alleviate it unless your lordship endeavours to keep still. It is most unfortunate that your lordship should be suffering from inflamed haemorrhoids and an attack of gout at one and the same time though I cannot help but observe that the latter affliction might in no small part be self-inflicted.'

'How dare you? I'll kick your arse!'

'I rather suspect that your lordship will be kicking nobody's arse in the immediate future.'

'Damn you, man! What the devil do you mean by "self-inflicted"?'

'Do you not think that the consumption of three bottles of port last evening might not have triggered the attack?'

'Hogwash! Nothing to do with it! It's genetic. Quacks have proved it.'

'If I may say so, I rather think the aetiology of the malady is not so clear cut.'

'What are you havering on about man? Speak English.'

'I doubt if your genetic history is the immediate cause.'

'Rot your guts, you imbecile, are you daring to contradict me?'

'In effect, yes.'

'You wouldn't have dared if I were well.'

'Almost certainly not.'

'Make a note in my day book to thrash you and then wring your scrawny neck as soon as I am recovered.'

'Very well, your lordship.'

'Three bottles of port! Three! Pah! Measly. I read somewhere that Dr Johnson used to drink three bottles of port *every night* after supper.'

'Boswell records *one* occasion where three bottles of port were consumed. They were shared on an evening when a large company of friends was gathered. That is rather different from your lordship's consuming three bottles of crusted port in two hours whilst binge-watching Peppa Pig.'

'There you go again!'

'Where do I go again?'

'Contradicting me.'

'Only because your lordship talks such arrant nonsense.'

'If I were you I would put your affairs in order because I swear on the bones of my ancestors that as soon as I am fit your days will be numbered - and we are talking single digits. What's the news?'

'The Prime Minister has announced that those living alone might meet up with another single person out of doors.'

'I don't want to go out of doors. It's been as hot as a poti's wengatami of late.'

'It is considerably cooler today, my lord, besides Lady Skellingthorpe has sent word that she intends to visit.'

'Put her off, man, put her off. I can't be seen like this. Spare me her fake solicitude. Just tell her politely to go to the devil.'

'Very good, my lord.'

'Now, I should like you to finish that dressing. Then I shall put my bum in a sling and you can cart me off to the quack.'

'I'm afraid that will not be possible.'

'There you go again! Contradicting me left, right and centre! Why will it not be possible, you festering abscess?'

'Because Dr Greetwell has closed down his surgery as a result of the pandemic. He is not seeing anyone.'

'He'll see me.'

'I must make bold to contradict your lordship again but he won't. He's gone away.'

'Where to? Lincoln? Grimsby? Don't tell me. Bugger's gone to Skegness, hasn't he? Living it up in Skeg-Vegas, eh?'

'No, your Lordship.'

'Where then, Dammit?'

'Jakarta.'

June 27th

'Callooh! Callay! O frabjous day! Come hither, Fiskers, my treasure, and let me kiss thee!'

'I would rather forgo that pleasure, if it is all the same to your lordship. What is the cause of this jubilation?'

'I read in *The Smellygraph* that pubs are to open from July 4th. Lay out my party togs, Fiskerton, my boy. Your Lord and master is off to ye Polecat for frolics and roistering.'

'I'm afraid that cannot be, your lordship. You and I are confined to barracks because of our age.'

'What about Washingborough? Is she allowed in the pub?'

'I do not know how old Mrs Washingborough is, your lordship. One does not ask a lady, no matter how lowly her station. However, I know that she is a lover of neither the grape nor the grain so she will scarcely be inconvenienced if her age debars her from visiting the inn.'

'What about Scampton?'

'I believe Scampton enjoys a pint or two of ale in the public bar on his annual day off, which he might choose to take soon, now that restrictions have been lifted somewhat.'

'Hmm. We'll see about that. Scopwick?'

'Scopwick is not yet fourteen, your lordship. On the other hand, one imagines that Major Saxilby of The Polecat would be only too happy to turn a blind eye to such a minor detail considering the blow to his revenue brought about the tavern's closure during lockdown. If the problem of the boy's stench could be overcome, of course.'

'Well, that is not going to be an issue for anybody. Chain up the gates after breakfast, Fiskerton. Don't forget the postern. If I am not allowed out, nor is anyone else.'

'That might be considered to be rather churlish by some, your lordship.'

'And would that "some" include yourself, Fiskerton.'

'I couldn't say, my lord.'

'Well, don't then.'

'My lord.'

'Now it says here that hairdressers can open too. I suppose I'm not allowed to visit my barber either.'

'That is correct.'

'But I am beginning to resemble the Wild Man of Borneo, am I not?'

'I must confess that your lordship is beginning to look decidedly hirsute.'

'And yet you are looking remarkably trim. What is your secret?'

'Mrs Washingborough was prevailed upon to give me a short back and sides, your lordship.'

'And something for the weekend?'

'Excuse me? I do not take your lordship's meaning.'

'Oh never mind. Do you think she might be prevailed upon to give the old baronial bonce a trim?'

'I think she would go into spasms of dread at the very suggestion, your lordship, and if I were to be perfectly candid I would have to say that, even if by some miracle she could be induced to come upstairs, I could not guarantee your lordship's safety were she to be wielding a pair of scissors.'

'Well, bother, you'll have to do it then. I can't go footling about the place looking like an old English sheepdog for much longer.'

'I have no expertise in the art, your lordship.'

'No matter. It is time for my summer plumage. Come along, Vidal Sassoon, collect your utensils and do your worst.'

July

July 4th

'What does it mean, Fiskerton? It says here in *The Telegraph* that face coverings will be required in shops.'

'Exactly what it says, your lordship. Some kind of face covering or mask will be required to minimise the spread of the virus.'

'Like Zorro, you mean?'

'No, not like Zorro.'

'Like the Lone Ranger?'

'No, not like the Lone Ranger. It is necessary just to cover the mouth and the nose to prevent the spread of the droplets which carry the virus.'

'Like the Phantom of the Opera?'

'No, that would be excessive and could alarm shop girls of a nervous disposition.'

'Like the Man in the Iron Mask?'

'Over the top. Just the mouth and nose, remember.'

'Like a bandit?'

'Precisely. You've got it. By Jove, you've got it!'

'Like a bank robber?'

'Just so. Like a bank robber.'

Pause

'Fiskerton?'

'Your lordship?'

'Do banks count as shops?'

'In what sense, my lord.'

'Will they be open? For business?'

'I believe so, your lordship.'

'But how will the cashiers be able to tell your common or garden customer wearing a face mask from a dangerous bank robber?'

'I believe that is something that the government may not have thought through to its logical conclusion.'

'I think so too. Do you know, Fiskerton, old banana. I feel a jolly jape coming on.'

'I'm afraid that your lordship must repress the urge. Those of us who are classified as clinically vulnerable as a result of our advanced years are not allowed out of our confinement until the first of August.'

'You are a frightful wet blanket, Fiskerton.'

'Indeed I am, sir. I am obliged to you for saying so.'

July 20th

'You know, Fiskers, *vieux haricot*, I don't mind telling you that I'm absolutely bored out of my tree.' This bally lockdown has been going on forever. I don't know what to do with myself.'

'A wise man once said that all human evil comes from a single cause, man's inability to sit still in a room.'

'Are you implying something, Fiskerton?'

'I would never be so presumptuous as to venture an implication, your Lordship.'

'I should think not.'

'Another wise man observed that an intelligent man is never bored.'

'Did he now? And where are they now, these wise men?'

'Dead, my lord.'

'Really? And do you not think there might not be a lesson for you in there somewhere?'

'Possibly. I do wish your lordship would stop brandishing the fire irons quite so menacingly.'

August

August 1st

'Well today's the day, eh, Fiskerton? Liberation Day! I have been so looking forward to this. Five months with nothing to look at but your dreary phizog. Enough to send a chap stark staring, eh? A little trip to the shops, see how the world wags, a whiz through the countryside and then a snifter or two in the old Polecat, what could be better, I say, what could be better?'

'I am so sorry to be the one to dampen your lordship's enthusiasm but there is something of a problem. I have just returned from the garage and am devastated to report that the Bentley will be going nowhere. The battery is quite dead after these months of desuetude.'

'These months of what? How many times do I have to tell you to speak English, man.'

'Lack of use, your lordship.'

'Well that's a bind, I must say. No matter - we'll take the Ford.'

'Same problem, I fear, your lordship.'

'The MG?'

'Ditto.'

'What about your Robin Reliant?'

'You made me sell it fifteen years ago, sir, to raise money for a bet at Market Rasen races.'

'Did I win?'

'No, your lordship. I did point out at the time that placing a bet on a horse called Casualty was asking for trouble but your lordship would not be gainsaid.'

'Well, I'll not be cheated of my little excursion. Do you know, I've never been to a supermarket. I am inordinately excited. There's nothing for it but to take a taxi. Order one immediately.'

'We shall need two, your lordship.'

'Why?'

'Because you will have to sit in the back wearing a face covering and it will not be possible for us to be socially distanced.'

'Socially distanced? What's that?'

'We need to be two metres apart.'

'What's a metre?'

'About six feet.'

'But we have been living in close proximity for as long as I can remember.'

'Indeed, but we shall be in public. It behoves your lordship, as a person of quality, to observe the protocols.'

'Be that as it may, there will be no second taxicab. Go and telephone for a single vehicle. You can follow on Scopwick's push bike.'

A little later

'Your taxi is here, my lord.'

'Where the devil have you been?'

'I have been fumigating the bicycle though I've not been wholly successful. A fetid air still hangs about it.'

'Yes, well never mind that. I will need a mask you say.'

'You will.'

'Do I have one?'

'Indeed you do, your lordship, and here it is. Made for you especially by Mrs Washingborough.'

'Yellow paisley?'

'Very fetching.'

'But won't I look a bit of a pansy?'

'Not in the least, your lordship. Look, it matches your cravat.'

'So it does.'

'You look every inch the country gentleman.'

'You think so?'

'Indeed you do. Though if I might venture the tiniest criticism.'

'If you think you dare.'

'It's hardly worth mentioning.'

'You're committed now.'

'It's the driving goggles, your lordship.'

'What about 'em?'

'Don't you think they might not appear a little superfluous in a minicab?'

'I do not - and, if you can't keep a civil tongue in your head, I'll trouble you to mind your own business in future. Superfluous indeed, pshaw!'

Much later

'What a god awful day, Fiskerton! I had no idea. You should have told me that a supermarket is a presage of what it would be like to be consigned to the nethermost circle of hell. Fat women flubbering about in their pyjamas with their goblin offspring in pushchairs because they're too fat or too lazy to walk…what are you coughing for, Fiskerton?'

'Frog in my throat, sir.'

'…and older children zooming about and getting underfoot with their faces covered in chocolate and snot, touching everything with their grubby mitts. And little hen-pecked men following meekly behind their wives as they load their trollies with crisps and biscuits and sweets and ice cream. And old codgers taking twenty minutes to choose a tin of beans when they're all the bloody same and standing in groups in the middle of the aisles and gossiping   and blocking the traffic and the queues and the noise - the NOISE!'

'Your lordship was not impressed then?'

'I was not. And then the audacity of it. That security guard who wouldn't let us out because we hadn't bought anything. I've got his number all right. I shall be writing to the manager. "Don't you know who I am?" I said. And what did he say? What did he say? He said: "I ain't got an effing clue, mush." What an oik! "I ain't got an effing clue." I'll have him.

'But as for The Polecat, the dear old Polecat. Oh, Fiskerton, the shock!'

'I was only too aware of your lordship's stupefaction and distress. Would your lordship like me to bring some tea?'

'No, I need something stronger. Cognac, I think. Large one. *Huge* one.'

'Of course.'

'But O, Fiskerton, The Polecat. Old Bob Saxilby sold up. Ruined by the virus. Moved to a little caff in Leighton Buzzard with that cantilevered barmaid. New management. What possessed them to brighten the place up like that? What was wrong with the gloom and the grime? That's what you need if you want to look after your regulars. You don't want to attract tourists and the like. Spoils the atmosphere.

'And what in the name of the Antichrist is a "gastropub"? Burgers? Ribs? Fries? And what the flute are nachos? What was wrong with the Major's steak and kidney pudding followed by jam roly-poly, eh? That's what I want to know. Nachos? What's wrong with a pickled egg and a packet of pork scratchings? Tell me that?

'And the place was seething with bloody children, running wild. There were even *babies*! Horrible things: faces like bags of spanners, gushing stinking effluvia from both ends. Herod knew what he was at, I tell you.

'World's gone to hell in a handcart. I predicted this nonsense when they started letting women into pubs. I knew no good would come of it.'

'I trust your lordship enjoyed the drive through the countryside at least?'

'I did not. I'd forgotten how boring the countryside is. Just fields. Nothing but fields.'

'And the occasional tree, your lordship.'

'Fields and the occasional tree. I say, Fiskerton.'

'Your lordship?'

'It's a bit early for the season but why don't I just shut this place up and make a beeline for Lindum House? I've suddenly developed a yen for a bit of London society. Start packing forthwith, Fiskerton.'

'I'm afraid that is not a viable proposition, your lordship.'

'Why do you flout my orders at every turn? Why ever not?'

'Because your lordship was obliged to sell the town house to pay your poker debts.'

'Ah yes. I'd forgotten that. When *was* that exactly?'

'Nineteen sixty-six.'

'I hear on the wireless that schools are to reopen in September, your lordship.'

'Excellent! Get the plankton off the streets and back in the jug again. Three Rs. *Amo, amas, amat.* History of the Empire. Spare the rod and spoil the child. Never did me any harm. Bit of roasting from time to time. Good for the soul. Instead of running amok on snake boards and eating burgers and spraying graffiti everywhere and calling it art.'

'Skateboards, your lordship.'

'What?'

'I believe they are called skateboards - not snake boards.'

'No, no, no, I assure you. It's snake boards. Take my word for it. Where were you at school, Fiskerton?'

'I never went to school, your lordship.'

'You never went to school?'

'I have been in your lordship's service since birth. I was a boot boy from the age of three, a page at seven, a footman at fourteen and I have been your lordship's valet and butler since 1960.'

'Good lord! But did your parents not want you to go to school.'

'I never knew my parents, your lordship.'

'But how did you come to be at Lindum Towers.'

'I have no idea, your lordship.'

'Extraordinary! Such loyalty should be rewarded.'

'Your lordship is too kind.'

'Steady on, man. I said it *should* be rewarded. Not that I was going to.'

August 29th
The Servant's Hall

'O Mr Fiskerton. Heaven help us all, what is that appalling noise?'

'I'm afraid his lordship is on the roof again, Mrs Washingborough.'

'Whatever is it this time?'

'It's to do with the fuss about slavery and the colonial history of the British Empire. He read in the newspaper that Rule Britannia and the other patriotic songs are to be played at the Last Night of the Proms but only in instrumental versions'

'O, that's a crying shame, Mr Fiskerton.'

'Shame? His lordship was incensed. He flung the teapot into the fire and hurled his breakfast egg at the portrait of his mother in the dining room. (Jolly good shot too.) Then he demanded to be taken up to the roof immediately.'

'But what is he doing? I thought it was the trump of doom.'

'Very nearly. In between blasts on his hunting horn and banging on a coal scuttle, he is singing through a megaphone. Thing is the songs are getting rather jumbled up:

sounds like *England's green and pleasant land of hope and glory rules the waves*. The tunes are rather mixed up too. Scopwick is marching up and down, with his lordship's encouragement, screeching some cacophonous descant and his lordship is so consumed with wrath that he doesn't even notice the pong.'

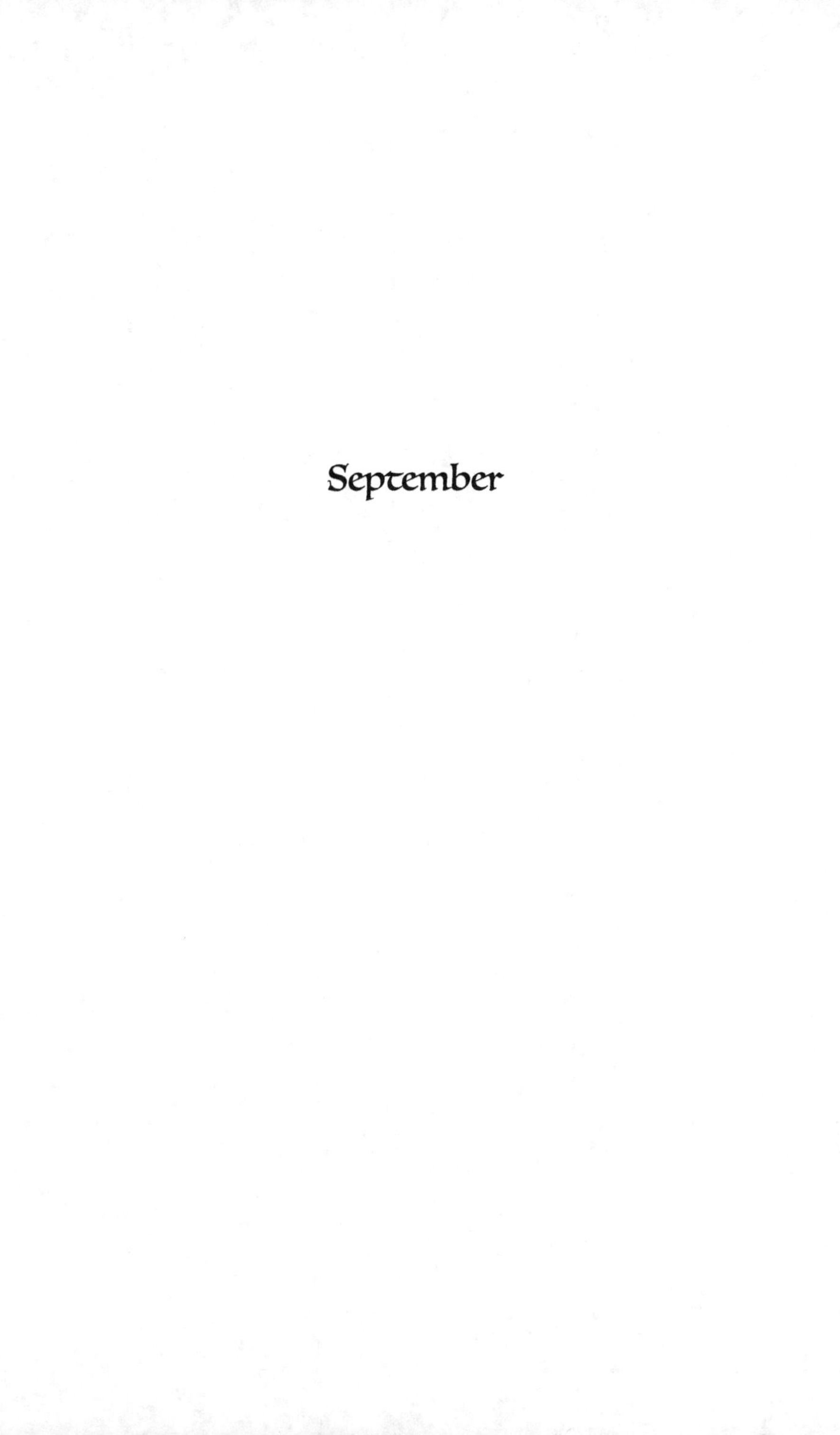

September

eptember 26th

'I must say this 10pm curfew doesn't make a lot of sense to me, Fiskerton.'

'Why so, your lordship?'

'Come now, any self-respecting landlord doesn't pay any attention to licensing hours, for God's sake. Old Major Saxilby never did. Opened up when he woke up - around three o'clock in the afternoon usually - called last orders around midnight - if your face didn't fit you were out on your Harris - if it did, you were fine. He'd bolt the door, close the curtains, and Bob's your uncle and Fifi's your aunt. Lockdown would sometimes last until dawn the next day. I remember once, there were just the Major, Canon Scothern and me. We kept on drinking for seventy-two hours - never opened up - just kept on drinking. Drained the place of gin and started in on the vodka.'

'All very well for a man of your lordship's constitution but hardly a recipe for the common man.'

'Ah, the common man is beyond hope. It says here in *The Torygraph* that "In cities such as York and Liverpool people thronged the streets after closing time, dancing and drinking from bottles; others fetched more from supermarkets."

'Where were the police, eh, Fiskerton, old stoat? Where were the mounted police? Where were the water cannon? Where were the tanks? By God, if I were a tad younger, I'd have ridden them down and horse-whipped the lot of them. Is there any more coffee?'

September 28th

'I see that Birmingham, Bolton, Greater Manchester, parts of Merseyside and parts of the North East have been placed under local restrictions.'

'How very unfortunate for them, your lordship.'

'Unfortunate? Have you taken leave of your senses? We're talking about the plebs here. They breed in places like that and spread all manner of diseases. Pity they can't all be isolated on the Isle of Man or something until this thing is over.'

'I doubt if that would be practicable, your lordship.'

'Why the devil not?'

'The logistics of transportation would be insuperable.'

'Bring in the army.'

'They wouldn't all fit.'

'You've no imagination, Fiskerton. 'That's your trouble, you know.'

September 29th

'Goodness gracious, Fiskerton. It doesn't do to skip the small print in *The Daily Telegraph*, you know. Look at this: 'A bone-eating vulture, *Gypaetus barbatus*, was spotted in Norfolk." What do you make of that, eh?'

'Not a great deal, your lordship.'

'Your bearded vulture is a very rare bird, Fiskerton, and I'm the one to bag the bugger. Think how splendid it would look under a glass dome in the library. Lay out my shooting jacket. We're off in an hour.'

'Impossible.'

'Why is it impossible? Car battery's fixed, isn't it?'

'Indeed, but does the article specify where the bird was spotted?'

'Not exactly.'

'No, and that is probably because the *rara avis* in question is a protected species.'

'How do you know all these things if you never went to school?'

'I select books from the library and read them under my haircloth blanket by torchlight. Your lordship does not permit me a light in my garret after nine o'clock.'

'Damn right. Now if protected status is all that's worrying you, forget it. Who's to know? Now dig out my cartridge bag and shooting stick, will you? Unless there's something else that's bothering you, that is?'

'Well there is, rather.'

'Spit it out.'

'There is the question of how we are to find this bird. Norfolk is quite a large county.'

'It's very flat.'

'All the same, the bird would need to be very large for one to be able to spot it at random.'

'How large? Bigger than Blackpool Tower.'

'Much bigger.'

'Bigger than the Empire State Building?'

'Infinitely. Besides, I would have the gravest difficulty manoeuvring your lordship's wheelchair over rough terrain.'

'A detail. Now, I'll need a tweed cap. The green herring-bone, I fancy.'

'Moreover, I just happen to know that Mrs Washingborough is making a Battenburg cake for elevenses.'

'Ah.'

'And you won't want to miss the Teletubbies, will you?'

'Er no. Scotch the plan. As you were, Fiskers. *Eh-oh.*'

October

O*ctober 9th*

'By the Lord Harry! Overlooked again!'

'What can your lordship mean? Overlooked by whom?'

'Her Britannic Majesty, Fiskerton.'

'How so?"

'The Queen's Birthday honours, man. Don't be obtuse.'

'But your lordship already has a title.'

'Yes but I looked to be made an earl at least. A dukedom wouldn't have gone amiss to be honest. Order of the Garter, that sort of thing.'

'Forgive me if I've missed the point but I have always been given to understand that in order to be in receipt of an honour one must be seen to have been of service to one's country or at least one's community.'

'Fiskerton, why do you always talk as if you had a plum in your mouth and a dictionary up your bum?'

'I believe it to be congruous with my position, your lordship.'

'Anyway, what the deuce do you mean? I am of service to the community. Do I not put a roof over the villagers' heads?'

'At prohibitive rents.'

'Eh? What was that? Speak up! Don't mutter, man!'

'So they don't live in tents.'

'Exactly. Besides look at the people who have been given honours. Dame Mary Berry? I ask you! I bet I could cobble together a Victoria sponge as well as her if I put my mind to it. Eh? Dame Maureen Lipman? Good lord! Any old fool can make a phone call. Sir David Suchet? He's not the only one with little grey cells, you know. A knighthood for Tommy Steel? God's knickers, what for? Being a cockney?

'So called entertainers - Pah! Whereas I, Fiskerton, contribute to the economy by employing people. Where would you be without my bounty, Fiskerton, and what about Washingborough, Scopwick and Scampton?'

'I shudder to think, my lord. Poor Scopwick wouldn't even have a piggery wherein to lay his flea-infested head.'

'Precisely.'

'Mind you, your father had upwards of thirty servants at the Towers in its hey-day: Upstairs maids, downstairs maids, in-between maids, a vegetable cook, a pastry cook, a scullery girl, grooms and flunkeys, stable boys and a chauffeur.'

'And it broke my heart to let them go, Fiskerton. One by one. But these are hard times and economies have had to be made.'

'I quite understand, your lordship.'

'Do you remember that excessively pretty parlourmaid, what was her name? Cherry Willingham, that was it. She was the first to go.'

'I do remember. Your father had to give her a solemn warning about spending so much time daydreaming in the cucumber patch. "I don't pay you to daydream in the cucumber patch," he said.'

'She didn't learn her lesson though, did she?'

'She did not. Your father had to let her go. He sent for her once and she didn't appear.'

'That was because I had her strapped to the bed, wasn't it?'

'Yes. "I don't pay you to be strapped to the bed," he said, when she'd finally been released. Scampton had to be sent for with bolt cutters. "Be off with you, you trollop,' your father said, 'and don't expect me to give you a character either."'

'Did she have to go on the game?'

'Fortunately not. The last I heard she was running a whelk stall in Mablethorpe.'

'Are you sure that isn't a euphemism, Fiskerton?'

'Not entirely, your lordship.'

'Happy days, eh?'

'Indeed.'

Still. This virus doesn't make things any easier. I fear there must be further salami slicing. At least one of you must go before Christmas.'

October 17th

'Explain this tier system to me, Fiskers, old partridge. Can't seem to get my head round it. Seems jolly potty, if you ask me.'

'As I understand it, the regions of England are placed in one of three tiers so that the relative prevalence of the virus is matched with corresponding restrictions. In Scotland, there are five tiers.'

'Why?'

'The First Minister likes to do the same as England, a little earlier or a little later, and with a slight variation. It is her principal way of demanding a second independence referendum.'

'I don't follow.'

'Nor does anyone else, your lordship.'

'Which tier are we in?'

'We are in tier 1, your lordship.'

'Is that good or bad?'

'It is the least restricted.'

'And how does that affect me.'

'Not at all, my lord. You are quite safe inside Lindum Towers.'

'I say, Fiskerton...'

'Your lordship?'

'There'll be tiers before bedtime, eh? what?'

'Most amusing.'

'But you're not laughing. You've got your morgue face on.'

'I can assure your lordship that, internally, I am convulsed.'

October 31st

'Your lordship must prepare himself. I bear bad news.'

'I can take it, Fiskerton. Give it to me raw. I shall show the same courage in adversity as I showed as a soldier of the Queen in the Second World War.'

'Soldier of the King.'

'Oh yes, the King. God rest his soul.'

'Your lordship was a child during the Second World War.'

'Was I? Oh yes. Well now, stop this beating about the bush, Fiskerton. What's your news?'

'Whilst your lordship was taking your nap, I heard on the wireless that because of the serious progress of the second wave the whole country is to be put in lockdown again.'

'Well, arse.'

'Indeed, my lord. However, there is a silver lining.'

'Which is?'

'The lockdown will only last until December 2nd.'

'Then what?'

'We return to the *status quo ante*.'

'The what?'
'The pre-existing state of affairs.'
'You mean it'll *end in tiers*?'
'Now that *is* rather comical, your lordship, I must admit.'
'I rather thought so.'

November

n**ovember 9th**

'Your Lordship! Your lordship!'

'What on earth is the matter, Fiskerton? Good lord, you have a button undone and your tie is crooked. Is it the end of the world?'

'No, your lordship. They've…'

'And there is a hair out of place, I swear. Help! It's the Apocalypse! Ragnarök is here! The moon is turning to blood! Run away! Doom!'

'No, no, no, it's good news! They've found a vaccine.'

'Eureka! They've found a vaccine! Does that mean I'll not be locked up any more.'

'Once the vaccine has been approved by the regulators and ready to be administered, that will eventually be the case, yes.'

'But I rather like being locked up.'

'But surely there is a difference between being confined because you want to be and being confined because you have to be?'

'There is indeed. *Magna Carta*, *Habeas Corpus*, *Carpe Diem* and all that. I know my rights. But Fiskerton, you rogue, I thought we already had a vaccine.'

'I'm sorry. I was unaware of that? Are you sure?'

'Bleach - you have to inject bleach. I heard President Trump saying you should inject bleach. Cleans your lav, after all - ought to flush out a pesky little virus, eh?'

'I fear the President was being rather absurd. No, a new vaccine has been developed by an American pharmaceutical concern called Pfizer.'

'You won't get rid of a virus with Tizer, old chum. Don't be preposterous.'

'No - Pfizer.'

'Oh right. Why didn't you say so? And who will be getting this vaccine first.'

'Front line services and then the elderly - oldest first.'

'That would be me then.'

'Yes, you'd be near the front of the queue.'

'How is it administered?'

'An injection into the muscle of the upper arm, I believe.'

'Oh, I don't like the sound of that. Still, better get it over with. Book me in for this afternoon.'

Advent 2020

December 1st
Advent Sunday

'Well, well, well, Fiskerton. I wonder if I can hazard a guess as to what it might be.'

'It shouldn't be too difficult, your lordship, given that today is Advent Sunday.'

'Is it? Is it really? Well, of course, we'd know that if we were allowed to go to church, wouldn't we?'

'Indubitably, though I cannot help pointing out that your lordship has not occupied the baronial box pew at St. Fiasco's since we regained the Falklands in 1982.'

'Be that as it may, I'm guessing that your little gift is an advent calendar. May I unwrap it? Ah yes, I was right as always. How charming! Now I believe that it is in order for me to open the first little door, is it not?'

'Indeed it is, your lordship.'

'Bless my soul, a miniature bottle of whisky. Now, would I be right in surmising that there is a miniature bottle of whisky behind each of the little doors?'

'Your lordship would be quite wrong, I'm afraid.'

'For once.'

'For once.'

'Do you see disappointment beginning to register on my face, Fiskerton?'

'It looks more like incipient rage to me, your lordship, but really there is no need.'

'Really? And why not?'

'Because behind each door there is a miniature bottle of a different kind of spirituous liquor.'

'That's more like it. This must have cost you a pretty penny, old boot?'

'I had to save for it for most of the year, my lord.'

'Did you? Did you really? All the same, I'm inclined to think I'm still paying you too much. Remind me to calculate your annual reduction in the New Year.'

'Your lordship is too gracious.'

'I am that. And, as further proof, I have an advent calendar for you too. Here.'

'But it is a thing of unimaginable beauty. Did your lordship make it yourself?'

'I did.'

'Now I understand why you locked yourself in the library all morning. I am deeply moved.'

'So you should be.'

'The painting is exquisite. I particularly like the flying cow.'

'The cow, Fiskerton, is Rudolph. Can't you tell from his red nose?'

'I beg your lordship's pardon. Of course it is. I was deceived by the udders. This is a breathtaking likeness of Mrs Washingborough waving a daffodil.'

'You obtuse oik, that's not Washingborough. It's the angel Gabriel with a trumpet.'

'Of course it is. Of course it is. I wondered why Mrs Washingborough was on the roof of the stable. Perhaps I'd better open the first window before I reveal any further artistic ineptitude.'

'I think that would be wise. You are making a bigger arse of yourself than usual.'

'Good heavens! It's a drawing of a mountain range! Stupendous!'

'Are you trying my patience on purpose? Whoever heard of mountain ranges in an advent calendar? It's a Toblerone, you clot!'

'So it is.'

'That's what you get in advent calendars, booze and chocolates.'

'Of course. I see it now. And are there chocolates behind all the windows?'

'Well, strictly speaking, no. There are *drawings of chocolates* behind all the windows. Now, I'd better be candid. I had a bit of trouble with the Toblerone - couldn't get the perspective quite right - so I thought I'd be a little less ambitious with the rest. There's a Smartie behind all the other windows.'

'I fear that that rather takes away the element of surprise that is usually considered definitive in the singular world of advent calendars.'

'Not in the least! I may have revealed the fact that there are Smarties behind each window, but you don't know the colour, do you? Ha! Got you there, haven't I? Now you're not going to say you'd have preferred real chocolates are you?'

'Certainly not! A real chocolate would have cost money. Very little, I grant you, but as for your drawings of chocolates, they must have taken time and genius!'

'They took simply ages. I was very keen not to go over the lines. That's how you can tell a great artist, you see. Did Leonardo da Vinci ever go over the lines? Did Titian? Did Tintoretto? Did Puccini? Of course they didn't!'

'I am somewhat overwhelmed to be the owner of such a masterpiece.'

'So you should be. Oh, by the way, I'm afraid the window for the 7th of December won't open. Had a bit of an accident with the gluepot. However, I'll tell you now, in order to avoid disappointment, the Smartie was brown.'

'My favourite colour, your lordship.'

Later

'It's perhaps a tad early but let's have the Christmas lights up 'ere long, Fiskerton. Dispel all the gloom and doom, shall we?'

'I shall put them up this evening. I know your lordship likes to play with the chase effects.'

'You're quite correct. I like the one where they all fade and you think: "Dash it! They're buggered - and then they go chasing each other all round the shop. Could watch 'em for hours.'

'I remember last year you watched for so long you became quite hypnotised, fell out of your chair and began miaowing like a cat.'

'I did, didn't I? Do you know, I'm feeling quite festive. I think I should like a glass of green ginger wine.'

'Very good, sir.'

'Is it time to start thinking of Christmas cards, do you suppose?'

'Your lordship does not send Christmas cards.'

'Do I not?'

'Not for many years. When the house was busier your lordship would send cards to all the staff, to the tenants and to your friends, informing them that on Christmas Eve you would be dressing up as Santa and would call on them to collect your presents.'

'By Jove, so I did.'

'When I endeavoured to point out that customarily Father Christmas is in the business of distributing presents rather than receiving them you made me stand in the middle of the frozen duck pond and pelted me with snowballs.'

'We had fun in those days, didn't we?'

'Indeed we did, sir.'

Thoughtful pause

'Bit of a bum year, 2020, eh what, Fiskerton, old bauble?'

'You could say that, your lordship. Without fear of contradiction, you could very well say that.'

'I just did.'

'So I observed, your lordship, very perspicacious of you.'

'Let's just hope 2021 turns out to be a bloody sight jollier.'

'Indeed, your lordship. Let us hope so.'

www.ingramcontent.com/pod-product-compliance
Lightning Source LLC
Chambersburg PA
CBHW061237140726
47998CB00006B/2018